THE FORCE AWAKENS: VOLUME 5

Luke Skywalker has vanished. In his absence, the sinister First Order has risen from the ashes of the Empire and will not rest until the last Jedi has been destroyed. The First Order and the Resistance are in desperate search of a map leading directly to Skywalker that is hidden inside the droid BB-8.

Finn, a former stormtrooper, and Rey, a young scavenger, become allies with the Resistance droid carrying the incomplete map to the missing Jedi, while befriending Rebellion heroes Han Solo and Chewbacca. After the group meets Han's mentor Maz Kanata on the planet Takodana, the First Order attacks and destroys everything in sight. The Resistance arrives to save the day, but not before Kylo Ren himself kidnaps Rey.

Now, it is up to Han Solo, Finn, and the Resistance to save Rey from the evil clutches of the First Order....

CHUCK WENDIG
Writer

LUKE ROSS
Artist

FRANK MARTIN
Colorist

VC's CLAYTON COWLES
Letterer

RAFAEL ALBUQUERQUE
Cover Artist

HEATHER ANTOS
Editor

JORDAN D. WHITE
Supervising Editor

C.B. CEBULSKI
Executive Editor

AXEL ALONSO
Editor In Chief

JOE QUESADA
Chief Creative Officer

DAN BUCKLEY
Publisher

Based on the screenplay by
LAWRENCE KASDAN & J.J. ABRAMS
and
MICHAEL ARNDT

For Lucasfilm:
Creative Director **MICHAEL SIGLAIN**
Senior Editor **FRANK PARISI**
Lucasfilm Story Group **RAYNE ROBERTS, PABLO HIDALGO, LELAND CHEE, MATT MARTIN**

ABDO
Spotlight

ABDOPUBLISHING.COM

Reinforced library bound edition published in 2018 by Spotlight,
a division of ABDO, PO Box 398166, Minneapolis, Minnesota 55439.
Spotlight produces high-quality reinforced library bound editions for
schools and libraries. Published by agreement with Marvel Characters, Inc.

Printed in the United States of America, North Mankato, Minnesota.
042017
092017

THIS BOOK CONTAINS
RECYCLED MATERIALS

marvelkids.com

PUBLISHER'S CATALOGING IN PUBLICATION DATA

Names: Wendig, Chuck, author. | Ross, Luke ; Martin, Frank ; Laming, Marc,
    illustrators.
Title: The force awakens / writer: Chuck Wendig ; art: Luke Ross ; Frank Martin ;
    Marc Laming.
Description: Reinforced library bound edition. | Minneapolis, Minnesota : Spotlight,
    2018. | Series: Star wars : the force awakens | Volumes 1, 2, 4, 5, and 6 written
    by Chuck Wendig ; illustrated by Luke Ross & Frank Martin. | Volume 3 written
    by Chuck Wendig ; illustrated by Marc Laming & Frank Martin.
Summary: Three decades after the Rebel Alliance destroyed the Galactic Empire, a
    stirring in the Force brings young scavenger Rey, deserting Stormtrooper Finn,
    ace pilot Poe, and dark apprentice Kylo Ren's lives crashing together as the
    awakening begins.
Identifiers: LCCN 2016961930 | ISBN 9781532140228 (volume 1) | ISBN
    9781532140235 (volume 2) | ISBN 9781532140242 (volume 3) | ISBN
    9781532140259 (volume 4) | ISBN 9781532140266 (volume 5) | ISBN
    9781532140273 (volume 6)
Subjects: LCSH: Star Wars fiction--Comic book, strips, etc.--Juvenile fiction. |
    Space warfare--Juvenile fiction. | Adventure and adventurers--Juvenile fiction. |
    Graphic novels--Juvenile fiction.
Classification: DDC 741.5--dc23
LC record available at https://lccn.loc.gov/2016961930

Spotlight

A Division of ABDO
abdopublishing.com

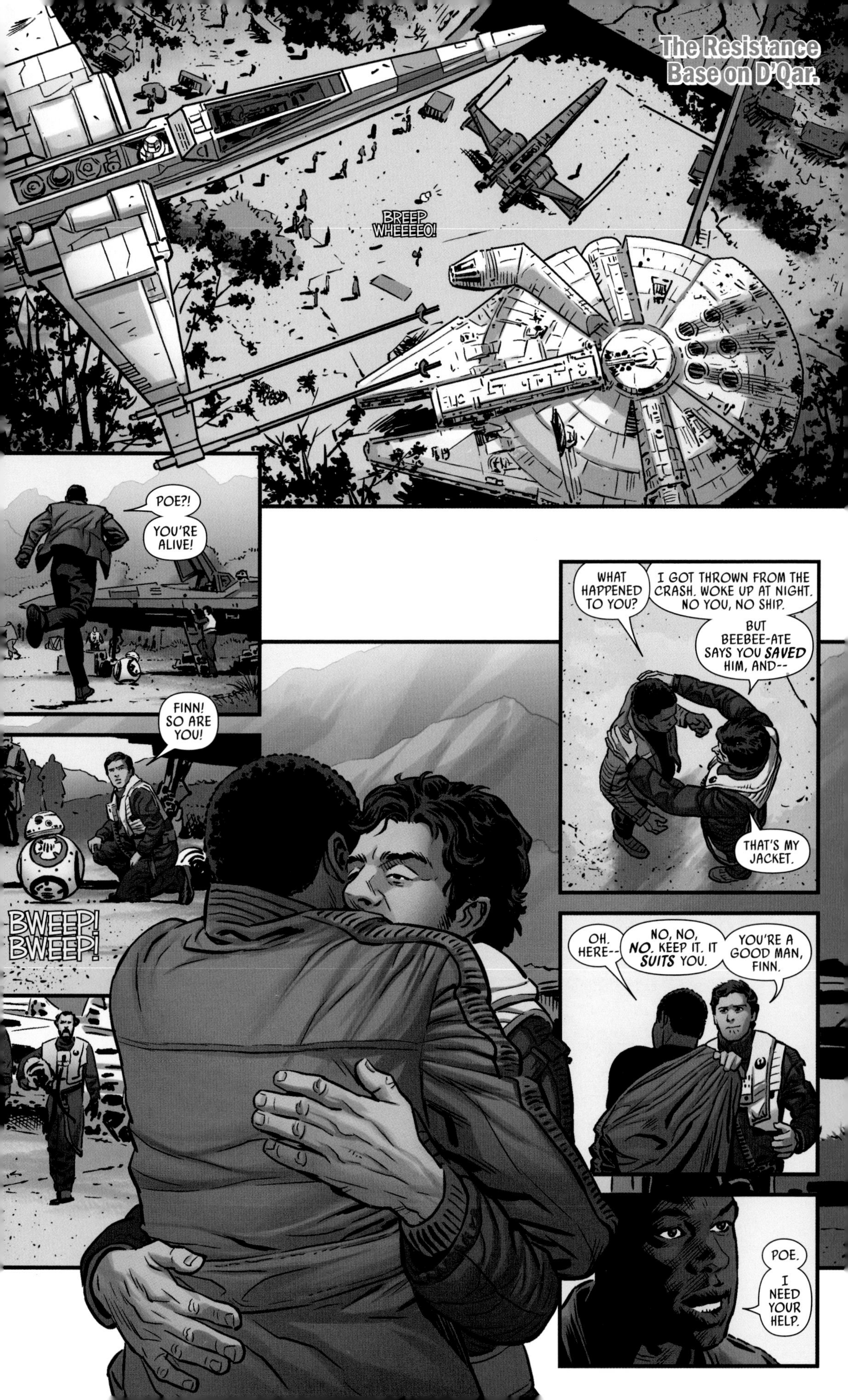
The Resistance Base on D'Qar.
BREEP WHEEEEO!
POE?!
YOU'RE ALIVE!
FINN! SO ARE YOU!
BWEEP! BWEEP!
WHAT HAPPENED TO YOU?
I GOT THROWN FROM THE CRASH. WOKE UP AT NIGHT. NO YOU, NO SHIP.
BUT BEEBEE-ATE SAYS YOU *SAVED* HIM, AND--
THAT'S MY JACKET.
OH. HERE--
NO, NO, *NO*. KEEP IT. IT *SUITS* YOU.
YOU'RE A GOOD MAN, FINN.
POE.
I NEED YOUR HELP.

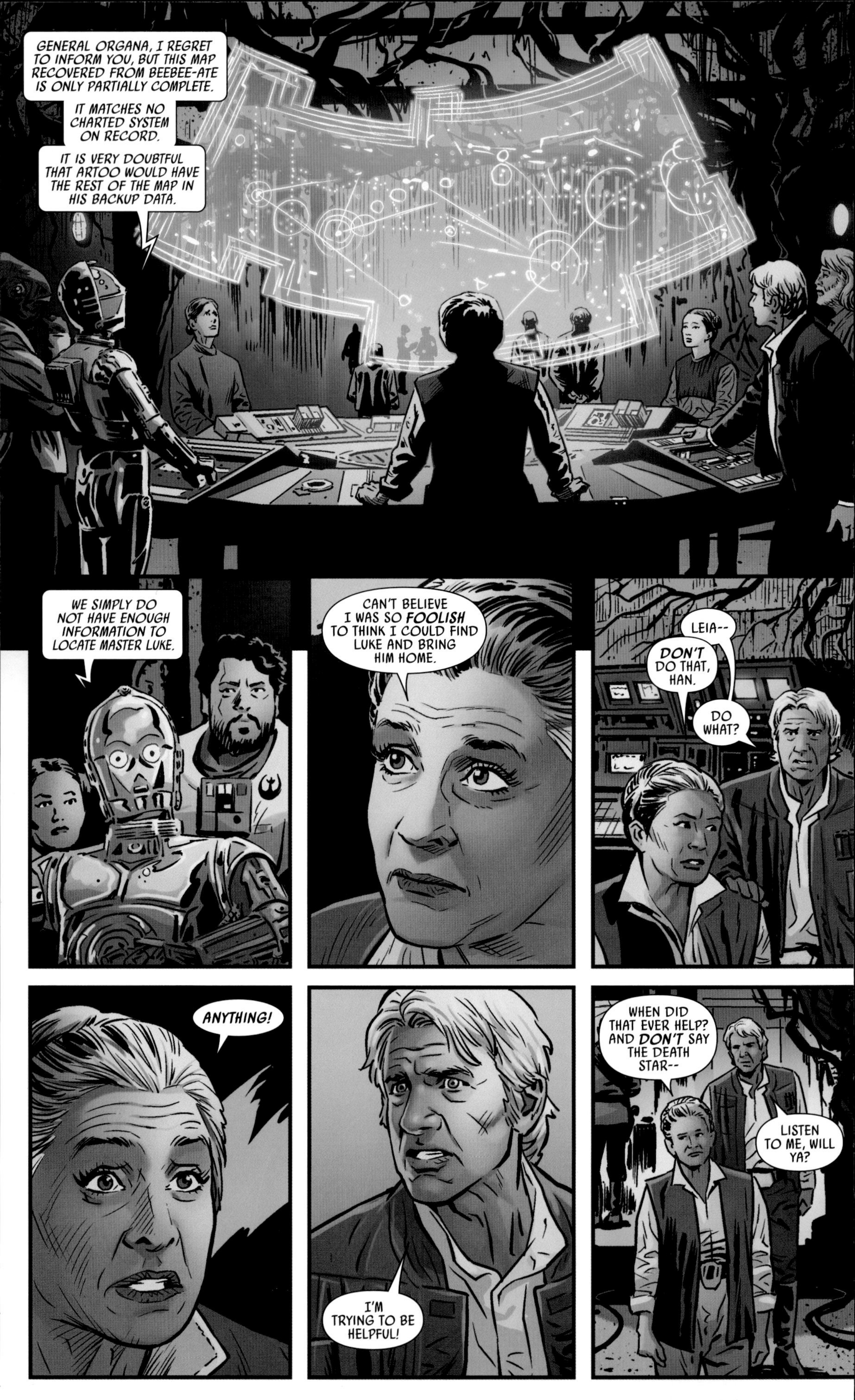
GENERAL ORGANA, I REGRET TO INFORM YOU, BUT THIS MAP RECOVERED FROM BEEBEE-ATE IS ONLY PARTIALLY COMPLETE.
IT MATCHES NO CHARTED SYSTEM ON RECORD.
IT IS VERY DOUBTFUL THAT ARTOO WOULD HAVE THE REST OF THE MAP IN HIS BACKUP DATA.
WE SIMPLY DO NOT HAVE ENOUGH INFORMATION TO LOCATE MASTER LUKE.
CAN'T BELIEVE I WAS SO FOOLISH TO THINK I COULD FIND LUKE AND BRING HIM HOME.
LEIA--
DON'T DO THAT, HAN.
DO WHAT?
ANYTHING!
I'M TRYING TO BE HELPFUL!
WHEN DID THAT EVER HELP? AND DON'T SAY THE DEATH STAR--
LISTEN TO ME, WILL YA?

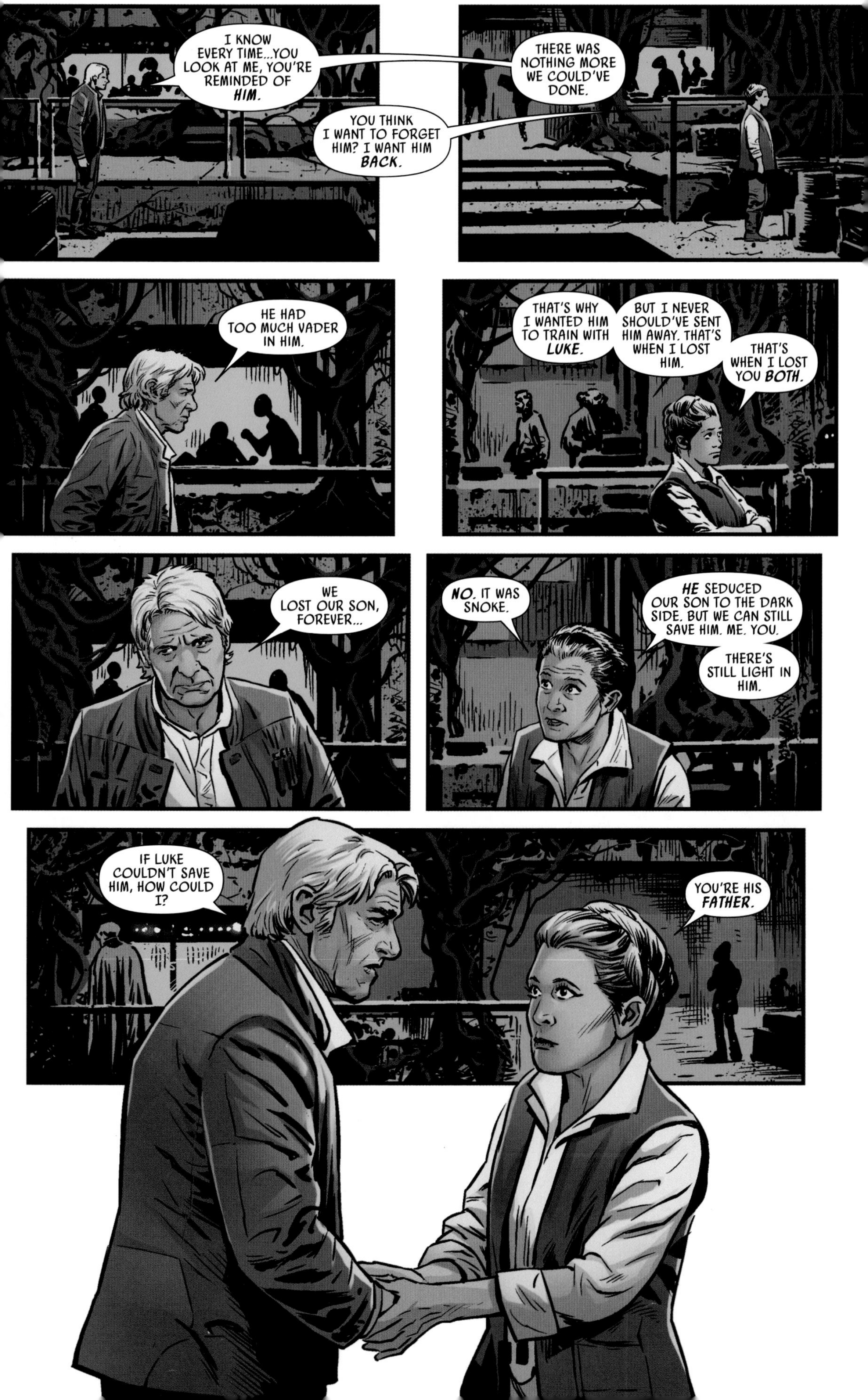
I KNOW EVERY TIME...YOU LOOK AT ME, YOU'RE REMINDED OF *HIM.*
THERE WAS NOTHING MORE WE COULD'VE DONE.
YOU THINK I WANT TO FORGET HIM? I WANT HIM *BACK.*
HE HAD TOO MUCH VADER IN HIM.
THAT'S WHY I WANTED HIM TO TRAIN WITH *LUKE.*
BUT I NEVER SHOULD'VE SENT HIM AWAY. THAT'S WHEN I LOST HIM.
THAT'S WHEN I LOST YOU *BOTH.*
WE LOST OUR SON, FOREVER...
NO. IT WAS SNOKE.
HE SEDUCED OUR SON TO THE DARK SIDE. BUT WE CAN STILL SAVE HIM. ME. YOU.
THERE'S STILL LIGHT IN HIM.
IF LUKE COULDN'T SAVE HIM, HOW COULD I?
YOU'RE HIS *FATHER.*

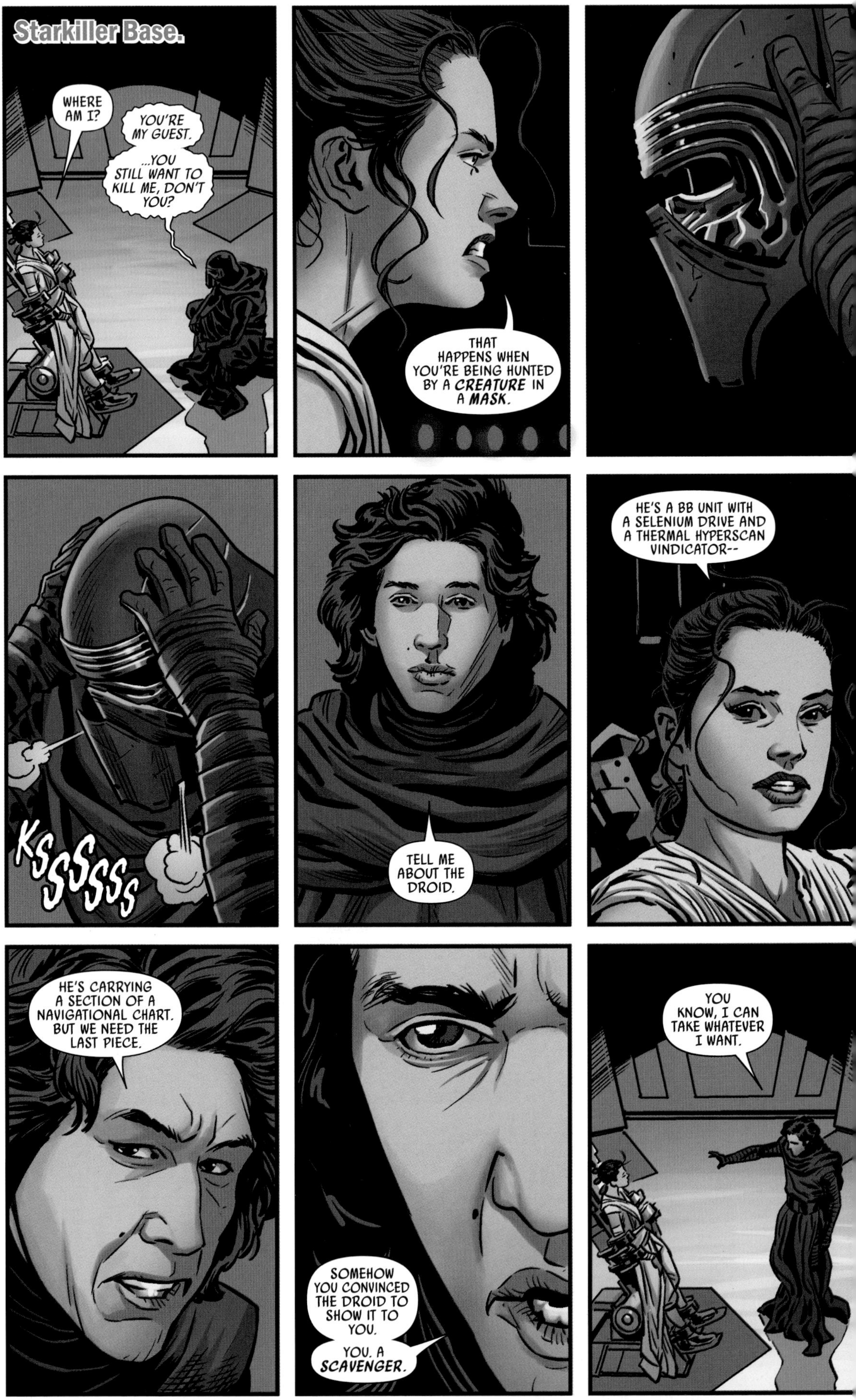
Starkiller Base.
WHERE AM I?
YOU'RE MY GUEST.
...YOU STILL WANT TO KILL ME, DON'T YOU?
THAT HAPPENS WHEN YOU'RE BEING HUNTED BY A CREATURE IN A MASK.
KSSSSSS
TELL ME ABOUT THE DROID.
HE'S A BB UNIT WITH A SELENIUM DRIVE AND A THERMAL HYPERSCAN VINDICATOR--
HE'S CARRYING A SECTION OF A NAVIGATIONAL CHART. BUT WE NEED THE LAST PIECE.
SOMEHOW YOU CONVINCED THE DROID TO SHOW IT TO YOU.
YOU. A SCAVENGER.
YOU KNOW, I CAN TAKE WHATEVER I WANT.

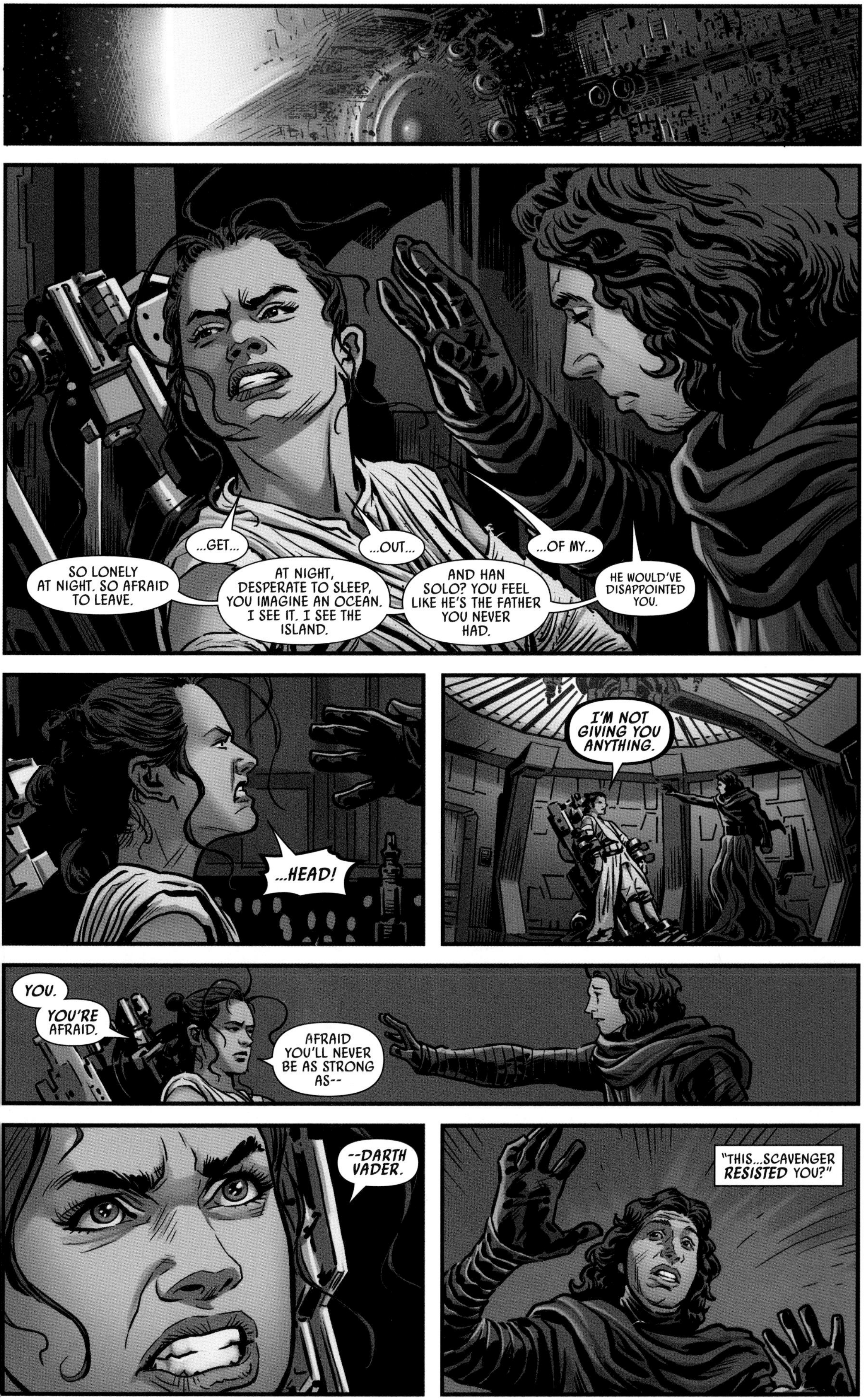
...GET...
SO LONELY AT NIGHT. SO AFRAID TO LEAVE.
...OUT...
AT NIGHT, DESPERATE TO SLEEP, YOU IMAGINE AN OCEAN. I SEE IT. I SEE THE ISLAND.
...OF MY...
AND HAN SOLO? YOU FEEL LIKE HE'S THE FATHER YOU NEVER HAD.
HE WOULD'VE DISAPPOINTED YOU.
...HEAD!
I'M NOT GIVING YOU ANYTHING.
YOU.
YOU'RE AFRAID.
AFRAID YOU'LL NEVER BE AS STRONG AS--
--DARTH VADER.
"THIS...SCAVENGER RESISTED YOU?"

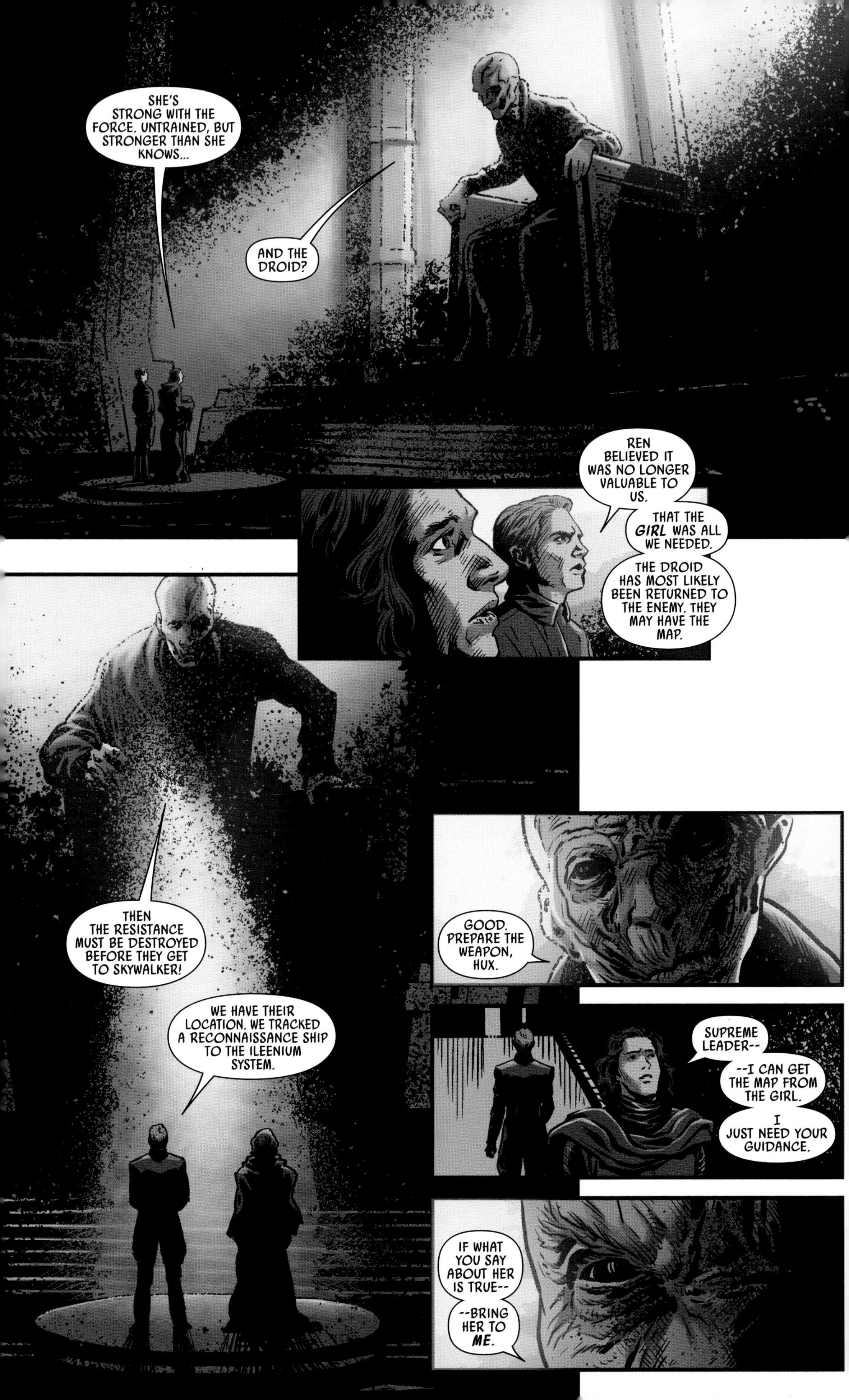
SHE'S STRONG WITH THE FORCE. UNTRAINED, BUT STRONGER THAN SHE KNOWS...
AND THE DROID?
REN BELIEVED IT WAS NO LONGER VALUABLE TO US.
THAT THE GIRL WAS ALL WE NEEDED.
THE DROID HAS MOST LIKELY BEEN RETURNED TO THE ENEMY. THEY MAY HAVE THE MAP.
THEN THE RESISTANCE MUST BE DESTROYED BEFORE THEY GET TO SKYWALKER!
WE HAVE THEIR LOCATION. WE TRACKED A RECONNAISSANCE SHIP TO THE ILEENIUM SYSTEM.
GOOD. PREPARE THE WEAPON, HUX.
SUPREME LEADER--
--I CAN GET THE MAP FROM THE GIRL.
I JUST NEED YOUR GUIDANCE.
IF WHAT YOU SAY ABOUT HER IS TRUE--
--BRING HER TO ME.

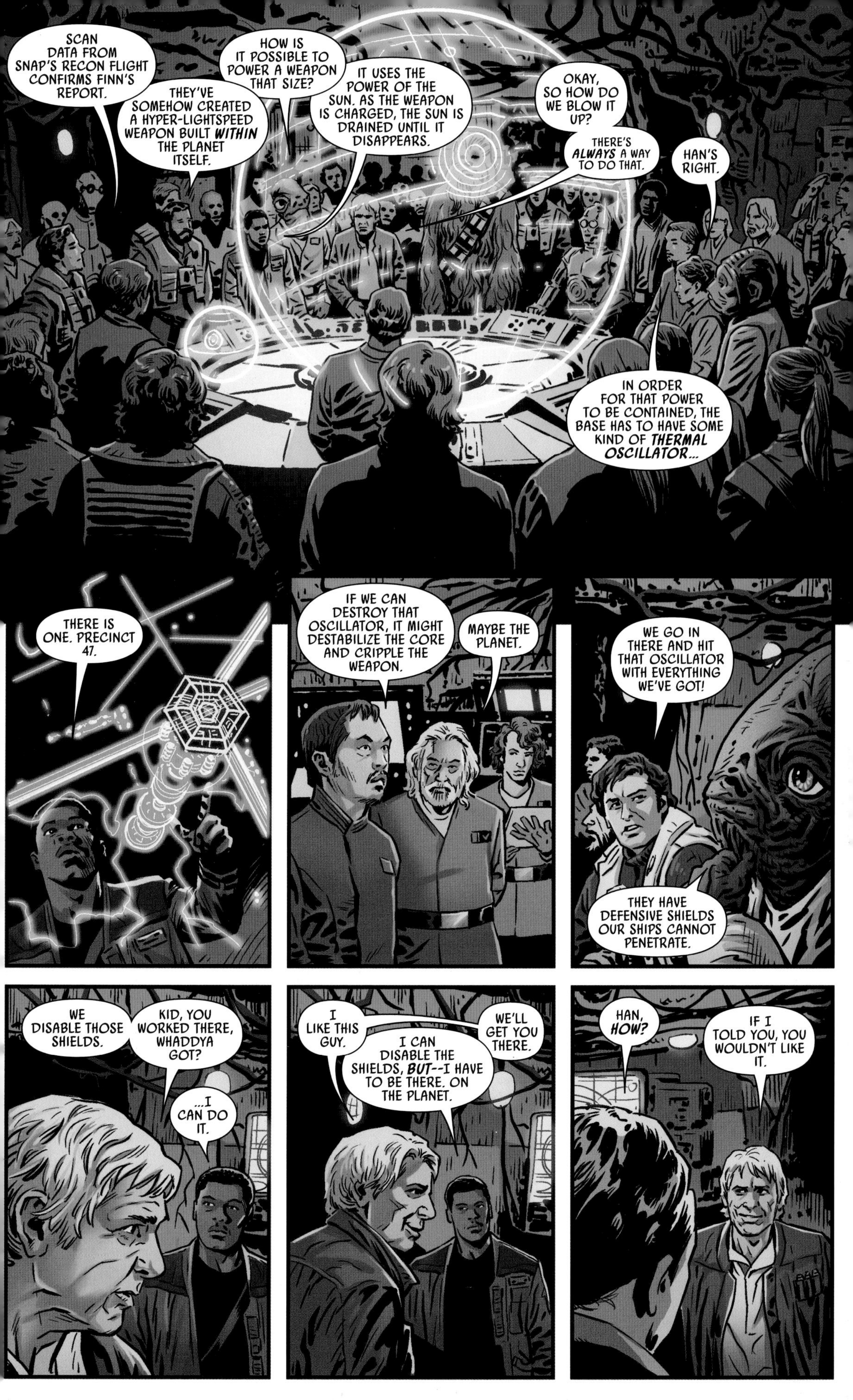
SCAN DATA FROM SNAP'S RECON FLIGHT CONFIRMS FINN'S REPORT.
THEY'VE SOMEHOW CREATED A HYPER-LIGHTSPEED WEAPON BUILT WITHIN THE PLANET ITSELF.
HOW IS IT POSSIBLE TO POWER A WEAPON THAT SIZE?
IT USES THE POWER OF THE SUN. AS THE WEAPON IS CHARGED, THE SUN IS DRAINED UNTIL IT DISAPPEARS.
OKAY, SO HOW DO WE BLOW IT UP?
THERE'S ALWAYS A WAY TO DO THAT.
HAN'S RIGHT.
IN ORDER FOR THAT POWER TO BE CONTAINED, THE BASE HAS TO HAVE SOME KIND OF THERMAL OSCILLATOR...
THERE IS ONE. PRECINCT 47.
IF WE CAN DESTROY THAT OSCILLATOR, IT MIGHT DESTABILIZE THE CORE AND CRIPPLE THE WEAPON.
MAYBE THE PLANET.
WE GO IN THERE AND HIT THAT OSCILLATOR WITH EVERYTHING WE'VE GOT!
THEY HAVE DEFENSIVE SHIELDS OUR SHIPS CANNOT PENETRATE.
WE DISABLE THOSE SHIELDS.
KID, YOU WORKED THERE, WHADDYA GOT?
...I CAN DO IT.
I LIKE THIS GUY.
WE'LL GET YOU THERE.
I CAN DISABLE THE SHIELDS, BUT--I HAVE TO BE THERE. ON THE PLANET.
HAN, HOW?
IF I TOLD YOU, YOU WOULDN'T LIKE IT.

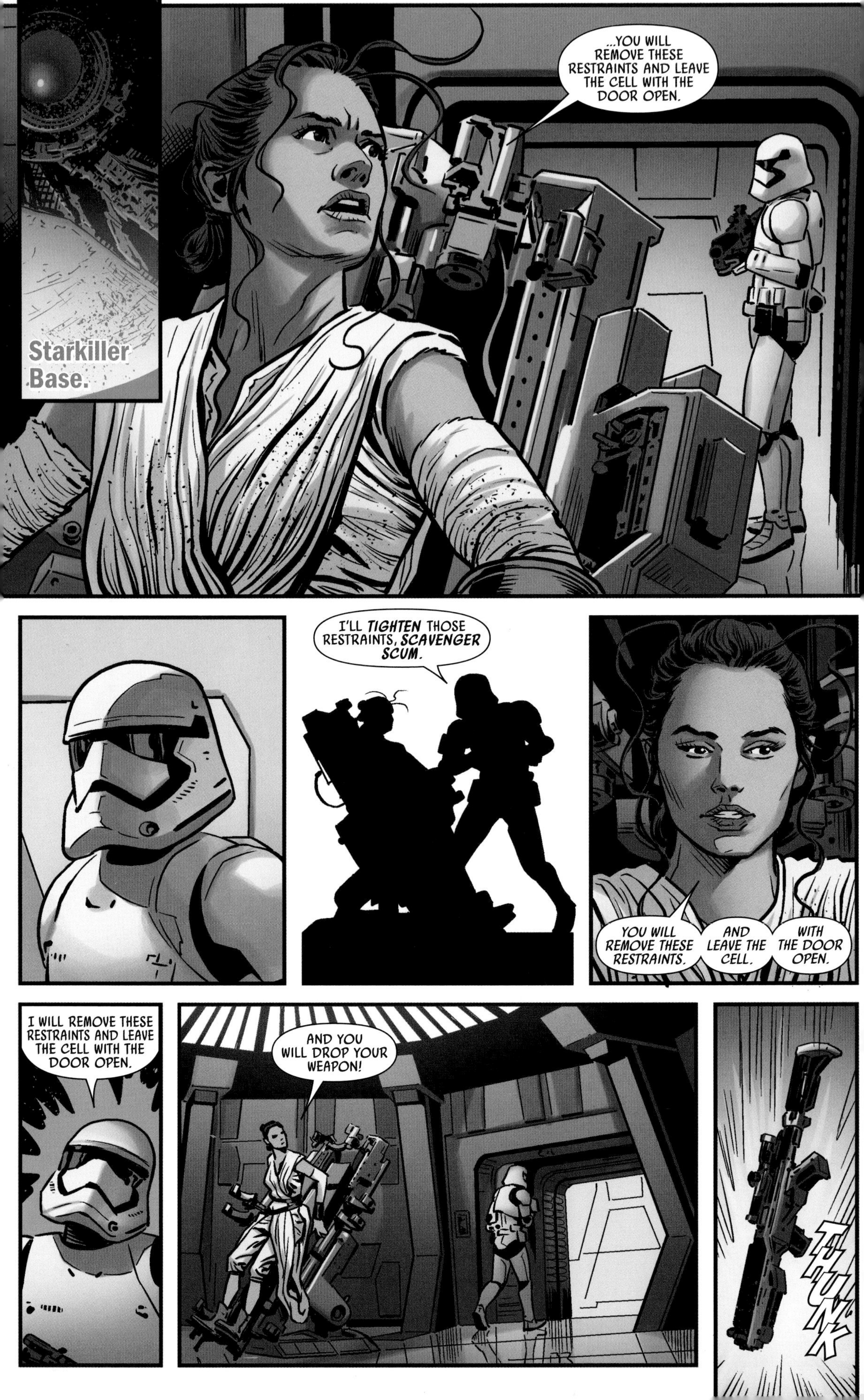
Starkiller Base.
...YOU WILL REMOVE THESE RESTRAINTS AND LEAVE THE CELL WITH THE DOOR OPEN.
I'LL TIGHTEN THOSE RESTRAINTS, SCAVENGER SCUM.
YOU WILL REMOVE THESE RESTRAINTS.
AND LEAVE THE CELL.
WITH THE DOOR OPEN.
I WILL REMOVE THESE RESTRAINTS AND LEAVE THE CELL WITH THE DOOR OPEN.
AND YOU WILL DROP YOUR WEAPON!
THUNK

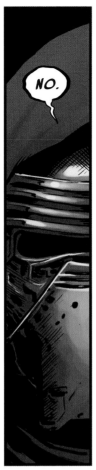

NO.

KZZZSH

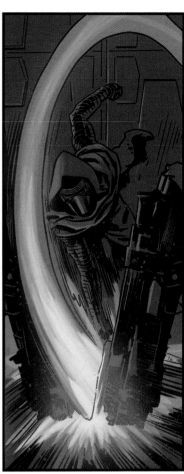

BEGIN CHARGING THE WEAPON!

YES, SIR. WEAPON CHARGING.

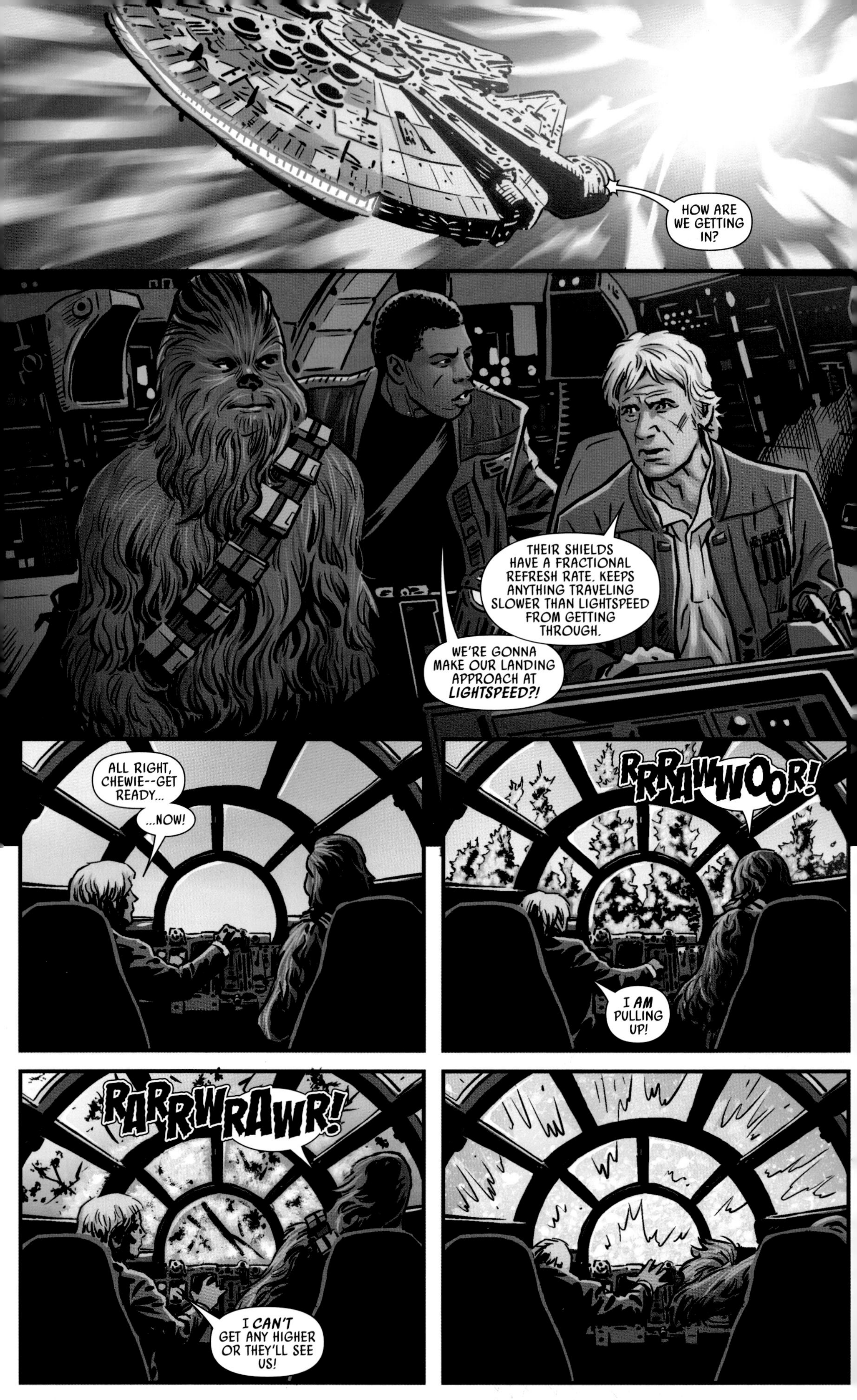
HOW ARE WE GETTING IN?
THEIR SHIELDS HAVE A FRACTIONAL REFRESH RATE. KEEPS ANYTHING TRAVELING SLOWER THAN LIGHTSPEED FROM GETTING THROUGH.
WE'RE GONNA MAKE OUR LANDING APPROACH AT LIGHTSPEED?!
ALL RIGHT, CHEWIE--GET READY...
...NOW!
RRRAWWOOR!
I AM PULLING UP!
RARRRWRAWR!
I CAN'T GET ANY HIGHER OR THEY'LL SEE US!

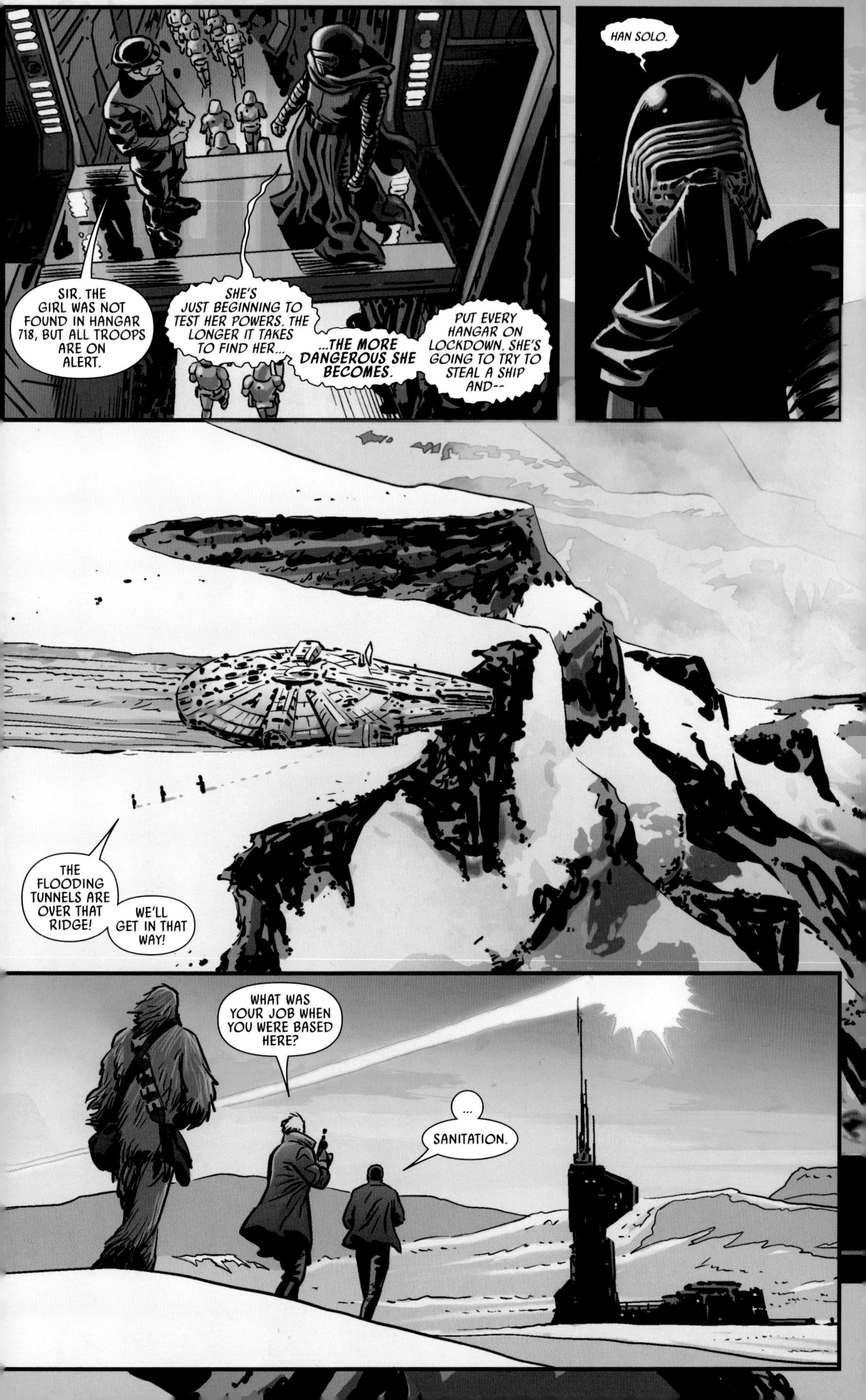
SIR. THE GIRL WAS NOT FOUND IN HANGAR 718, BUT ALL TROOPS ARE ON ALERT.
SHE'S JUST BEGINNING TO TEST HER POWERS. THE LONGER IT TAKES TO FIND HER...
...THE MORE DANGEROUS SHE BECOMES.
PUT EVERY HANGAR ON LOCKDOWN. SHE'S GOING TO TRY TO STEAL A SHIP AND--
HAN SOLO.
THE FLOODING TUNNELS ARE OVER THAT RIDGE!
WE'LL GET IN THAT WAY!
WHAT WAS YOUR JOB WHEN YOU WERE BASED HERE?
...
SANITATION.

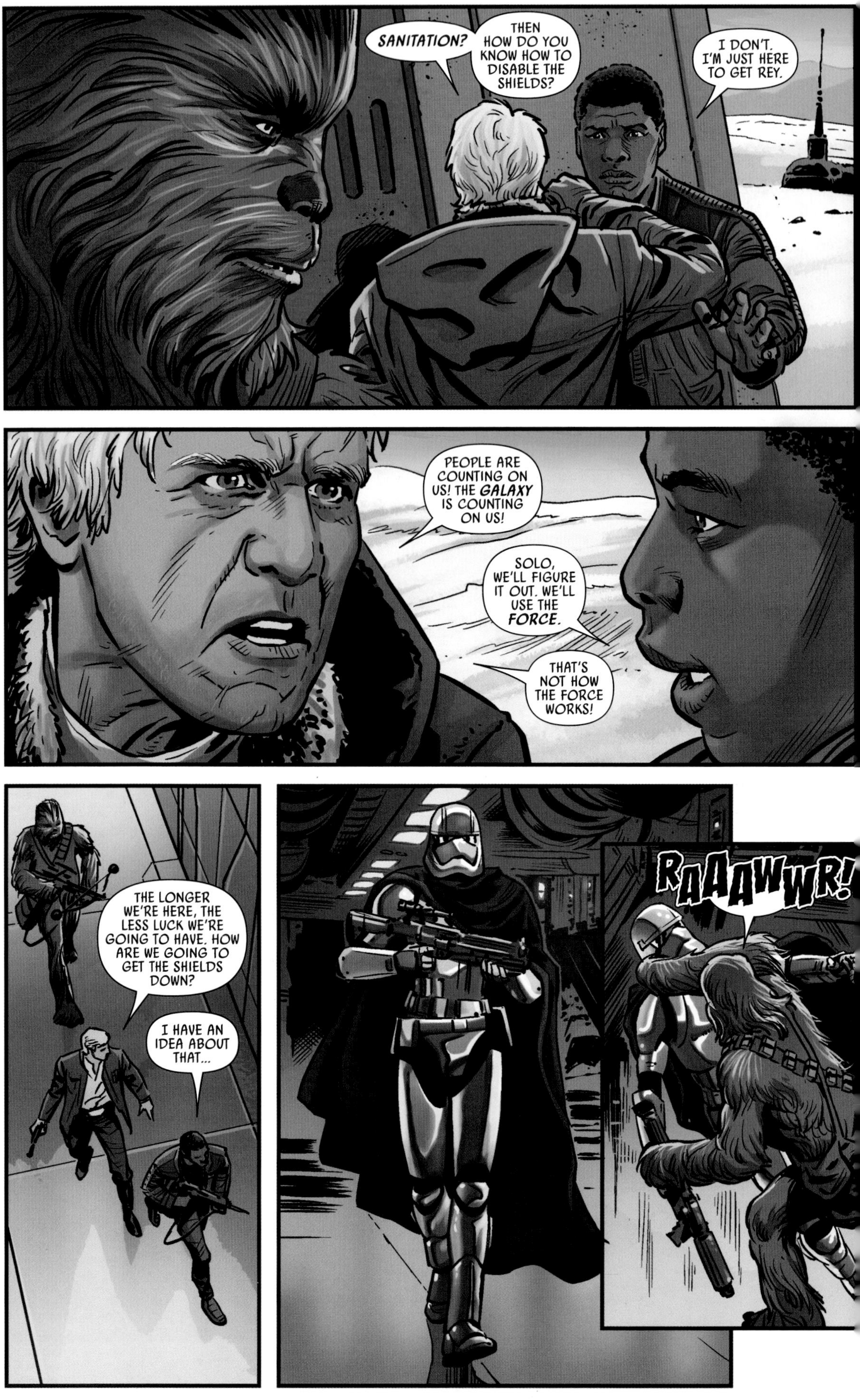
SANITATION?
THEN HOW DO YOU KNOW HOW TO DISABLE THE SHIELDS?
I DON'T. I'M JUST HERE TO GET REY.
PEOPLE ARE COUNTING ON US! THE GALAXY IS COUNTING ON US!
SOLO, WE'LL FIGURE IT OUT. WE'LL USE THE FORCE.
THAT'S NOT HOW THE FORCE WORKS!
THE LONGER WE'RE HERE, THE LESS LUCK WE'RE GOING TO HAVE. HOW ARE WE GOING TO GET THE SHIELDS DOWN?
I HAVE AN IDEA ABOUT THAT...
RAAAWWR!

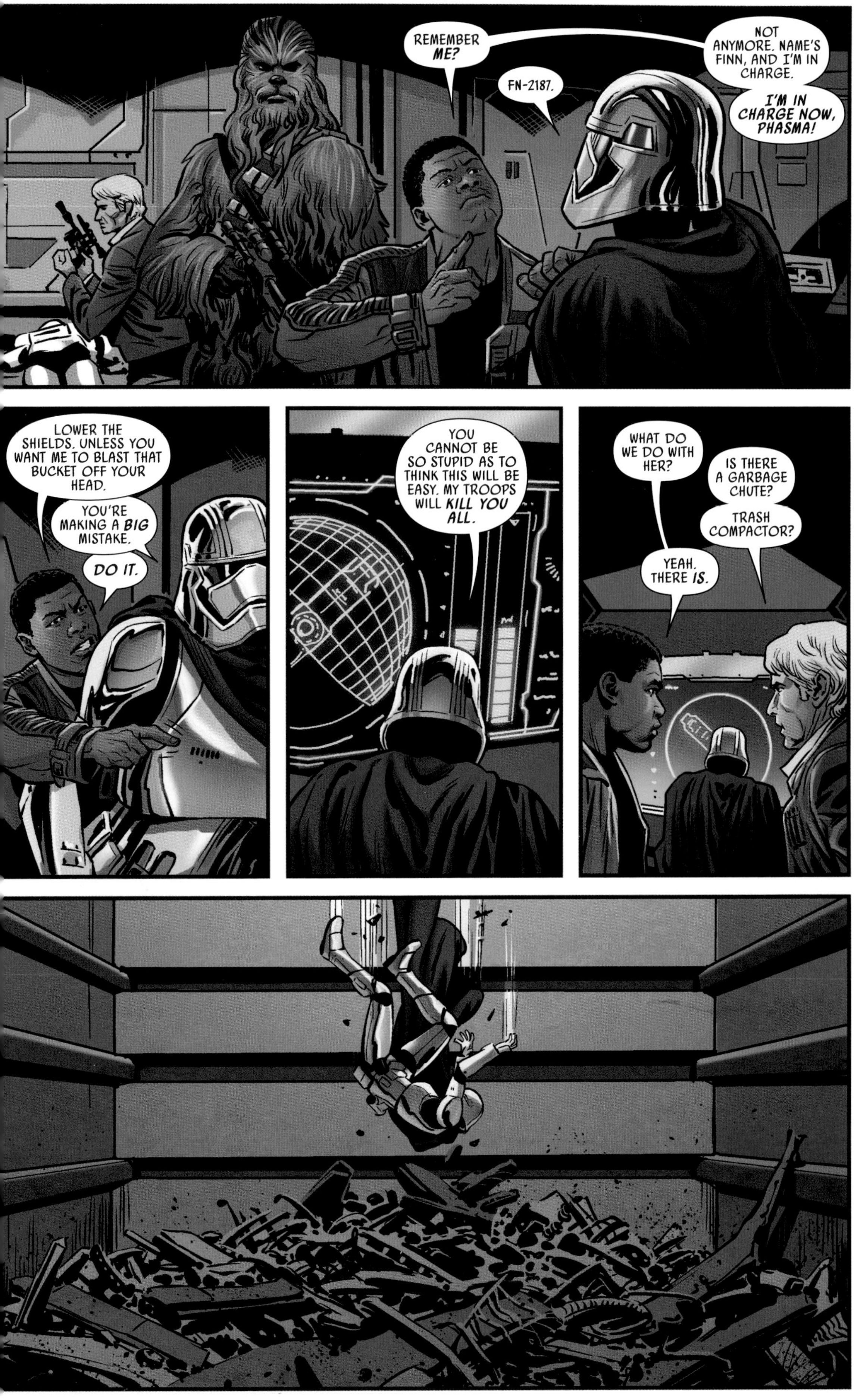
REMEMBER ME?
FN-2187.
NOT ANYMORE. NAME'S FINN, AND I'M IN CHARGE.
I'M IN CHARGE NOW, PHASMA!
LOWER THE SHIELDS. UNLESS YOU WANT ME TO BLAST THAT BUCKET OFF YOUR HEAD.
YOU'RE MAKING A BIG MISTAKE.
DO IT.
YOU CANNOT BE SO STUPID AS TO THINK THIS WILL BE EASY. MY TROOPS WILL KILL YOU ALL.
WHAT DO WE DO WITH HER?
IS THERE A GARBAGE CHUTE?
TRASH COMPACTOR?
YEAH. THERE IS.

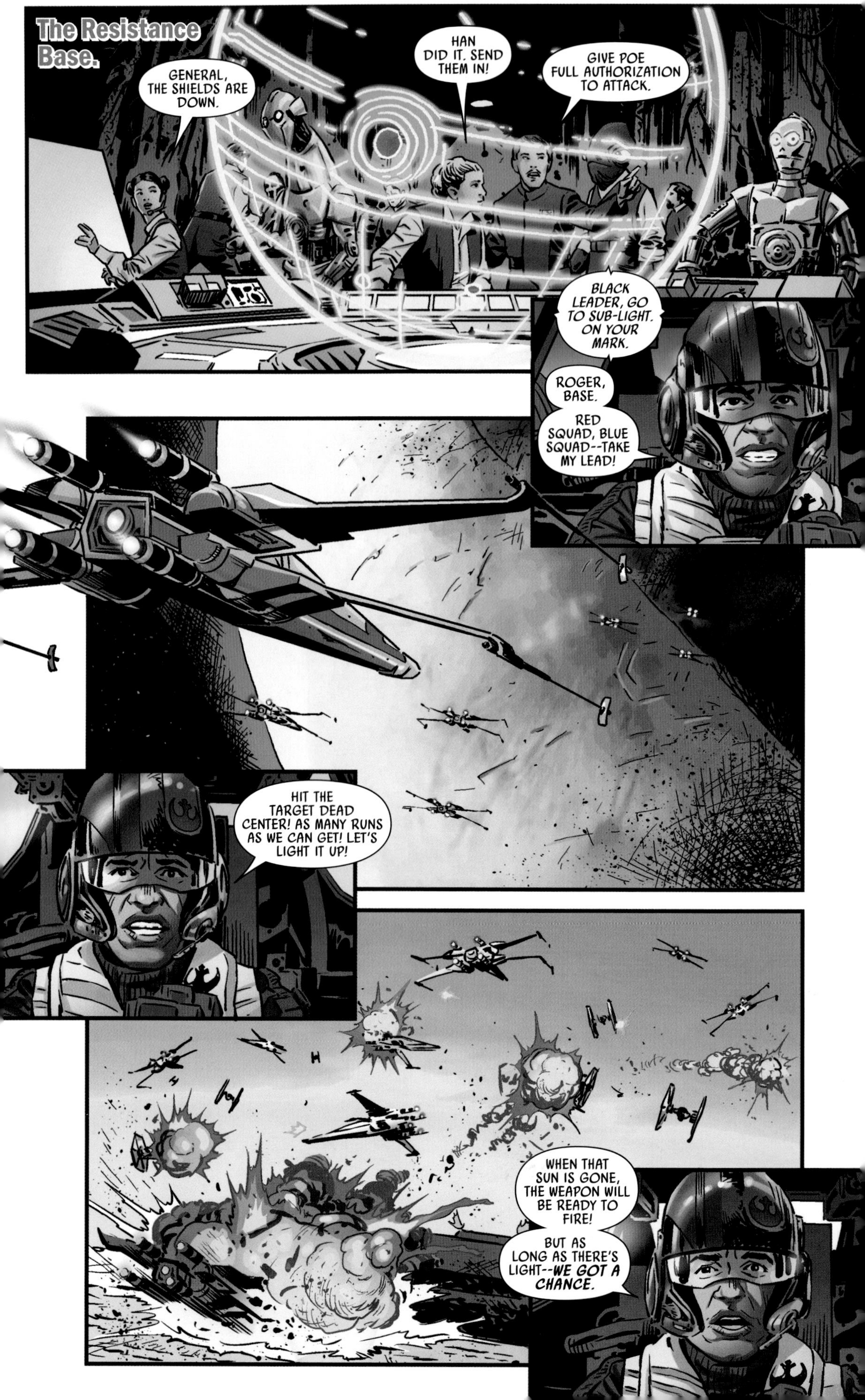
The Resistance Base.
GENERAL, THE SHIELDS ARE DOWN.
HAN DID IT. SEND THEM IN!
GIVE POE FULL AUTHORIZATION TO ATTACK.
BLACK LEADER, GO TO SUB-LIGHT. ON YOUR MARK.
ROGER, BASE.
RED SQUAD, BLUE SQUAD--TAKE MY LEAD!
HIT THE TARGET DEAD CENTER! AS MANY RUNS AS WE CAN GET! LET'S LIGHT IT UP!
WHEN THAT SUN IS GONE, THE WEAPON WILL BE READY TO FIRE!
BUT AS LONG AS THERE'S LIGHT--*WE GOT A CHANCE.*

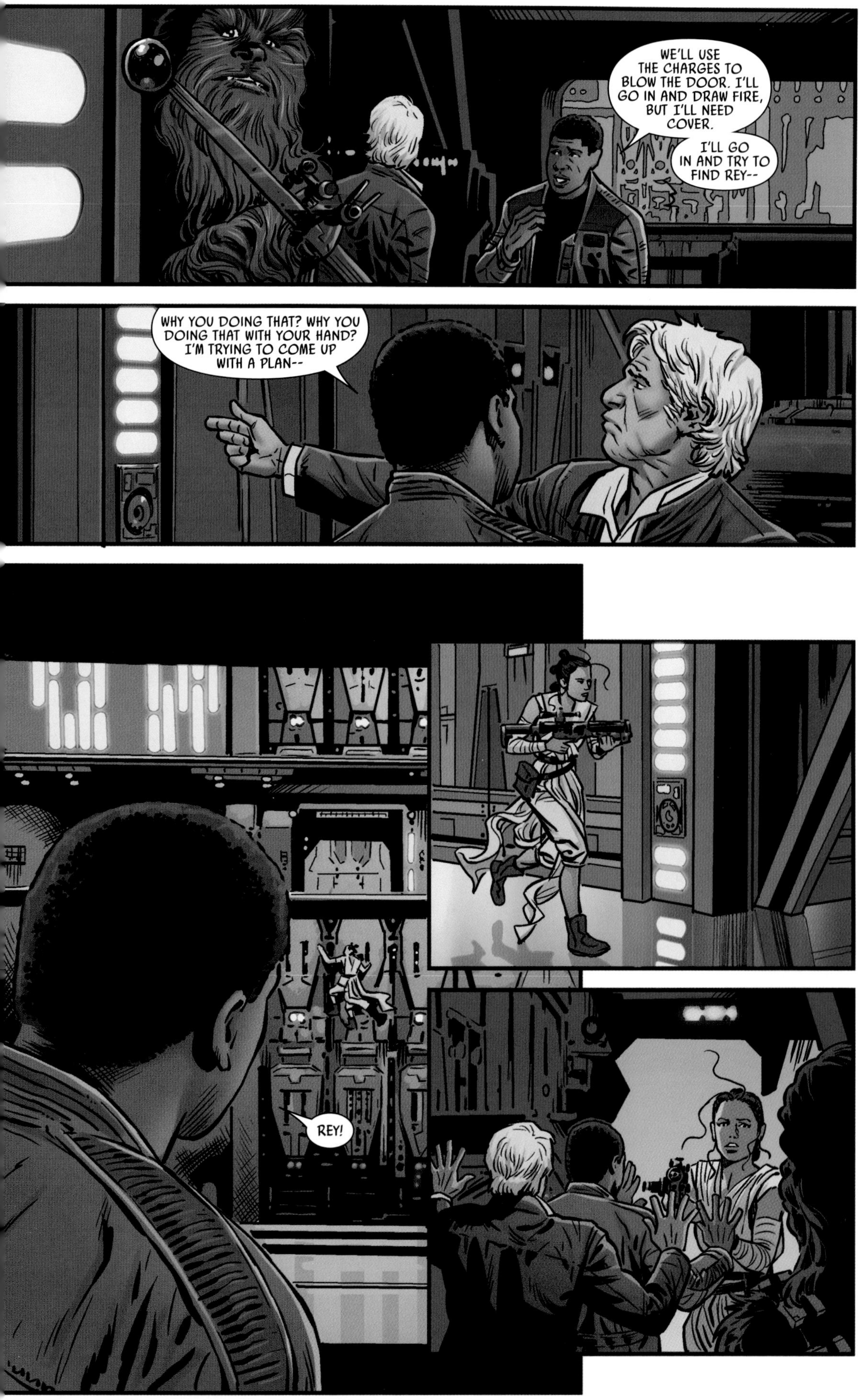
WE'LL USE THE CHARGES TO BLOW THE DOOR. I'LL GO IN AND DRAW FIRE, BUT I'LL NEED COVER.
I'LL GO IN AND TRY TO FIND REY--
WHY YOU DOING THAT? WHY YOU DOING THAT WITH YOUR HAND? I'M TRYING TO COME UP WITH A PLAN--
REY!

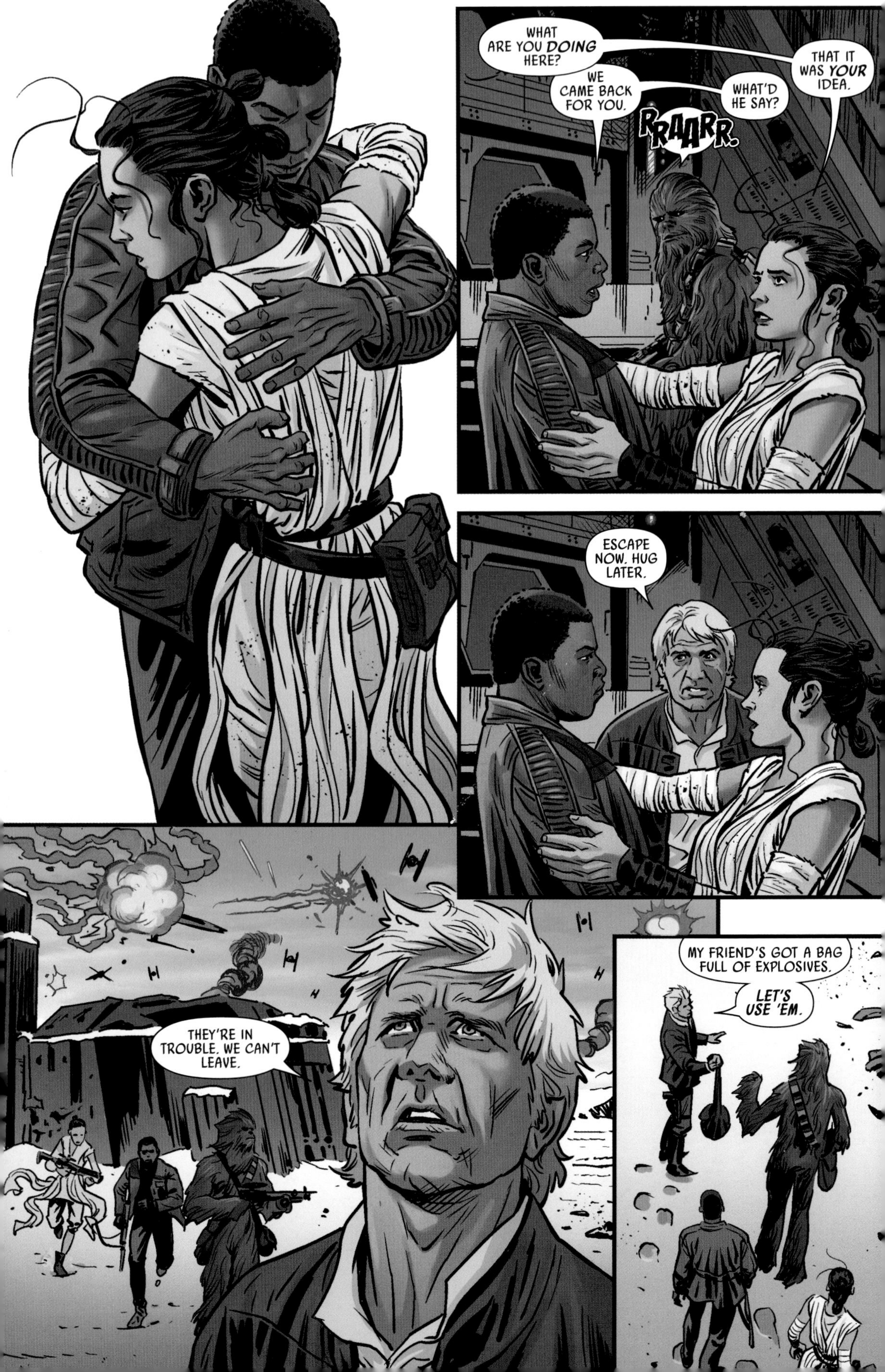
WHAT ARE YOU DOING HERE?
WE CAME BACK FOR YOU.
RRAARR.
WHAT'D HE SAY?
THAT IT WAS YOUR IDEA.
ESCAPE NOW. HUG LATER.
THEY'RE IN TROUBLE. WE CAN'T LEAVE.
MY FRIEND'S GOT A BAG FULL OF EXPLOSIVES.
LET'S USE 'EM.

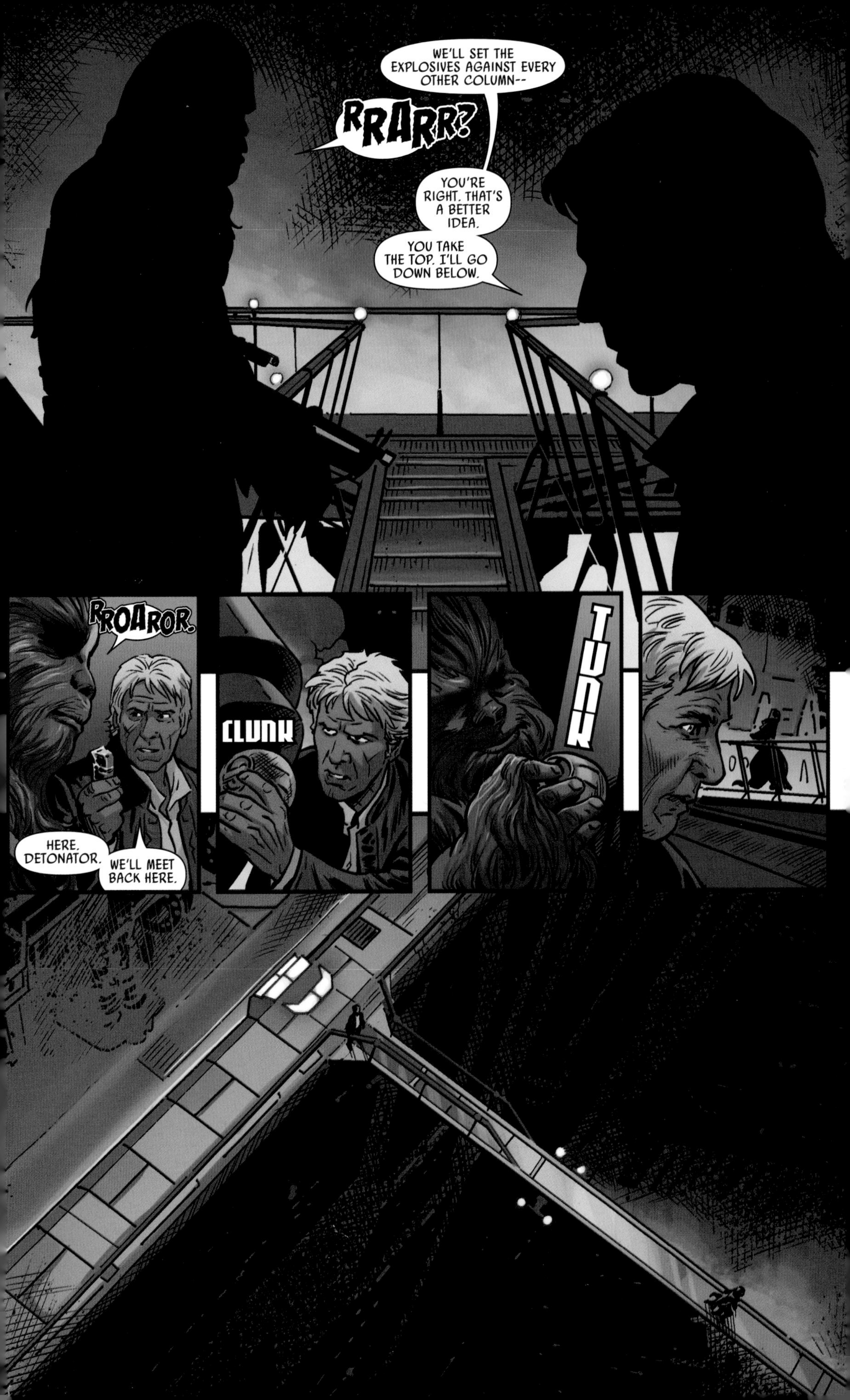
WE'LL SET THE EXPLOSIVES AGAINST EVERY OTHER COLUMN--
RRARR?
YOU'RE RIGHT. THAT'S A BETTER IDEA.
YOU TAKE THE TOP. I'LL GO DOWN BELOW.
RROAROR.
HERE. DETONATOR.
WE'LL MEET BACK HERE.
CLUNK
TUNK

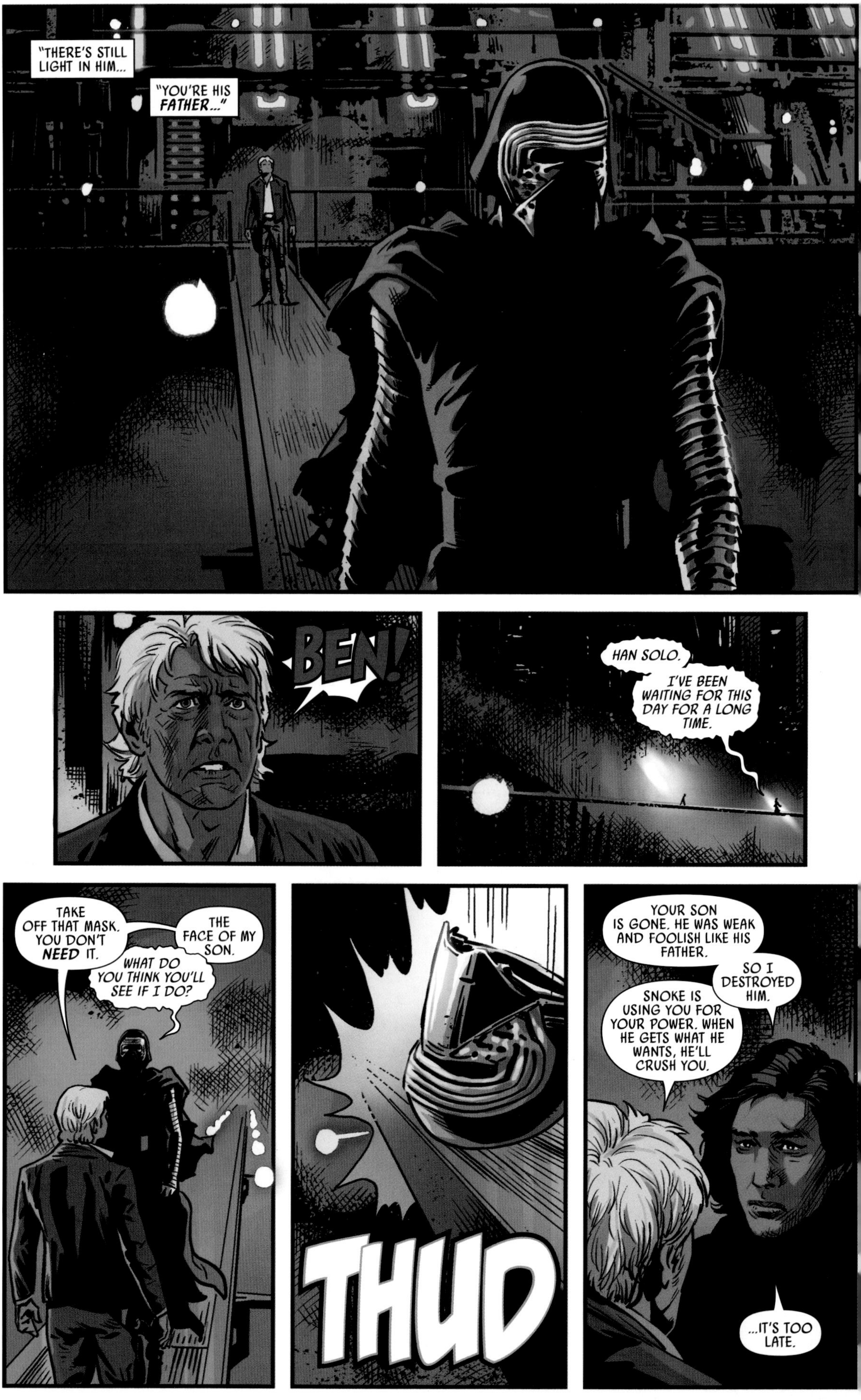

"THERE'S STILL LIGHT IN HIM...
"YOU'RE HIS *FATHER*..."
BEN!
HAN SOLO.
I'VE BEEN WAITING FOR THIS DAY FOR A LONG TIME.
TAKE OFF THAT MASK. YOU DON'T **NEED** IT.
WHAT DO YOU THINK YOU'LL SEE IF I DO?
THE FACE OF MY SON.
THUD
YOUR SON IS GONE. HE WAS WEAK AND FOOLISH LIKE HIS FATHER.
SO I DESTROYED HIM.
SNOKE IS USING YOU FOR YOUR POWER. WHEN HE GETS WHAT HE WANTS, HE'LL CRUSH YOU.
...IT'S TOO LATE.

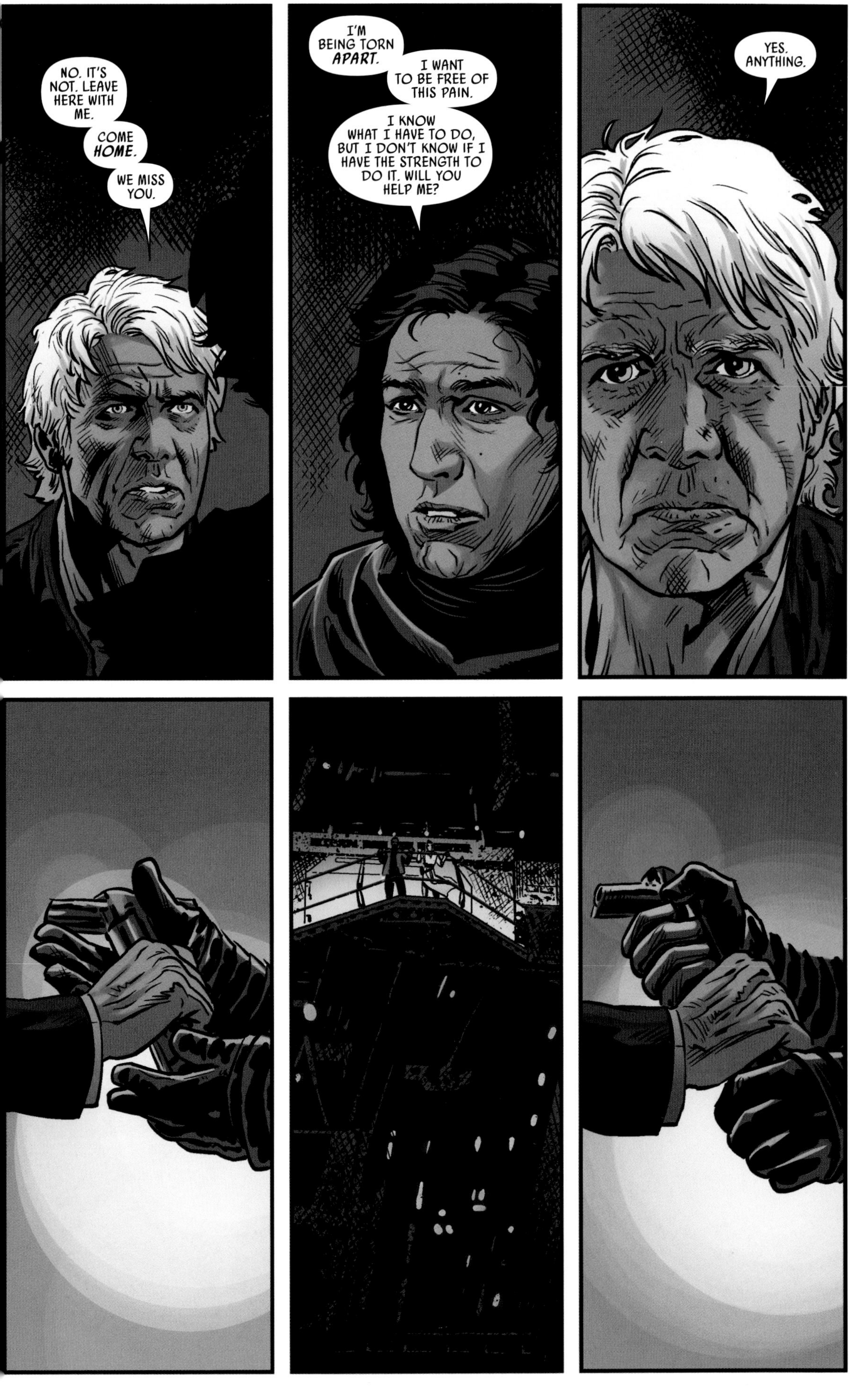
NO. IT'S NOT. LEAVE HERE WITH ME.
COME HOME.
WE MISS YOU.
I'M BEING TORN APART.
I WANT TO BE FREE OF THIS PAIN.
I KNOW WHAT I HAVE TO DO, BUT I DON'T KNOW IF I HAVE THE STRENGTH TO DO IT. WILL YOU HELP ME?
YES. ANYTHING.

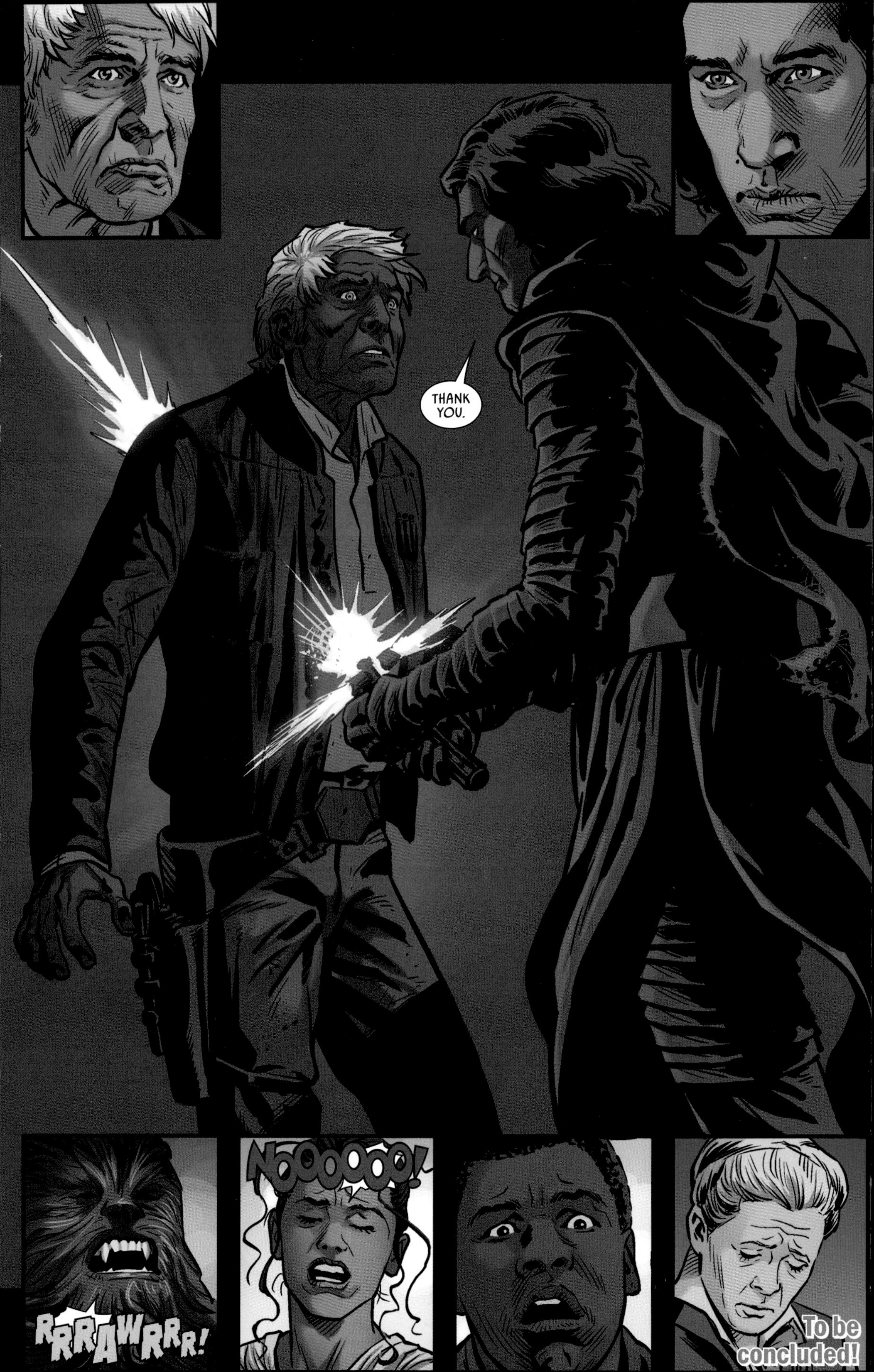
THANK YOU.
NOOOOOO!
RRRAWRRR!
To be concluded!

STAR WARS
THE FORCE AWAKENS

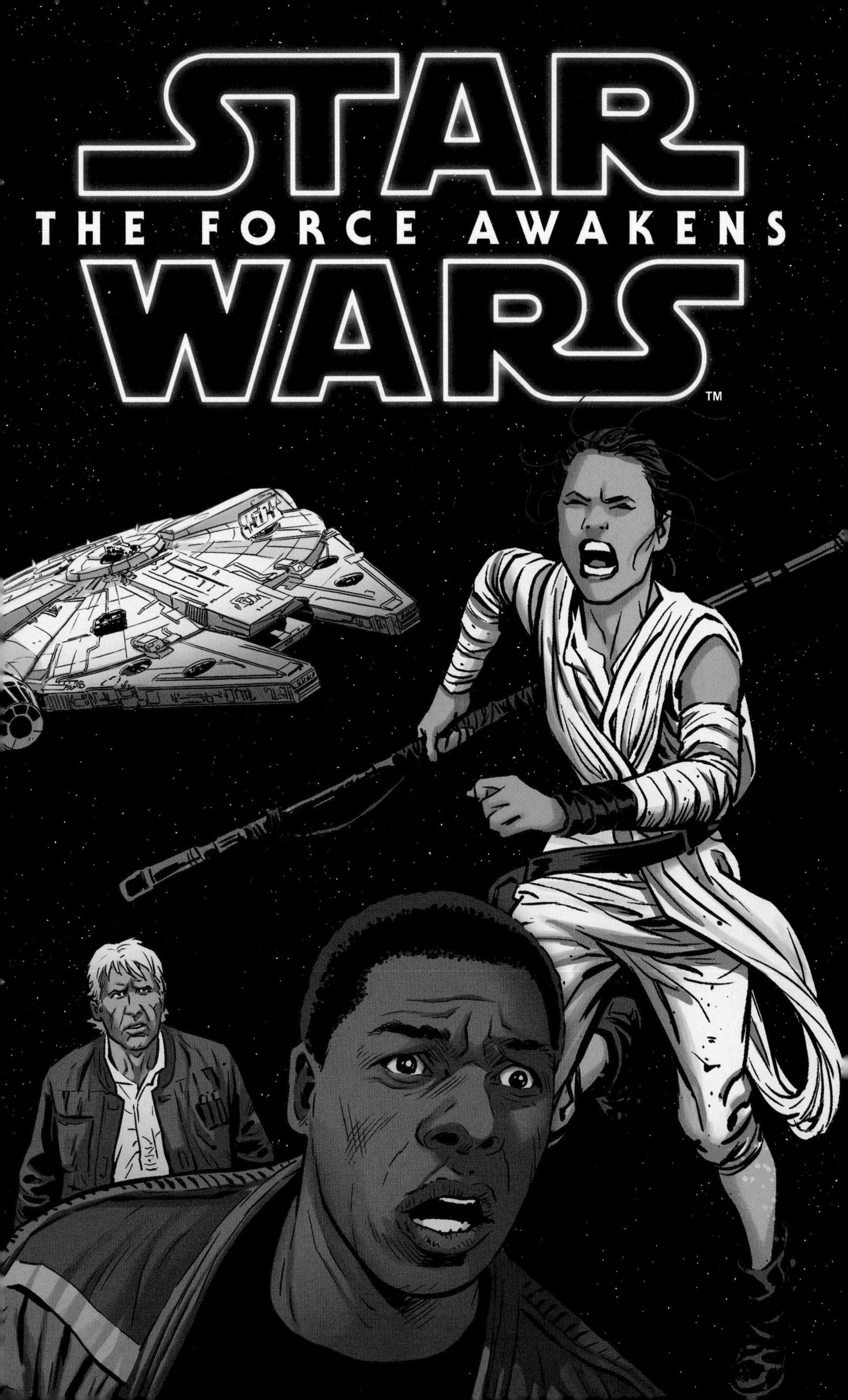

STAR WARS
THE FORCE AWAKENS

TM

COLLECT THEM ALL!

Set of 6 Hardcover Books ISBN: 978-1-5321-4021-1

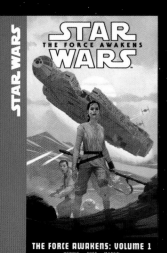

STAR WARS
STAR WARS
THE FORCE AWAKENS
THE FORCE AWAKENS: VOLUME 1
WENDIG ROSS MARTIN

Hardcover Book ISBN
978-1-5321-4022-8

STAR WARS
STAR WARS
THE FORCE AWAKENS
THE FORCE AWAKENS: VOLUME 2
WENDIG ROSS MARTIN

Hardcover Book ISBN
978-1-5321-4023-5

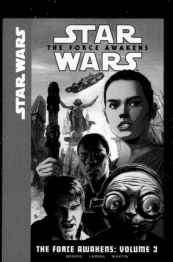

STAR WARS
STAR WARS
THE FORCE AWAKENS
THE FORCE AWAKENS: VOLUME 3
WENDIG LAMING MARTIN

Hardcover Book ISBN
978-1-5321-4024-2

STAR WARS
STAR WARS
THE FORCE AWAKENS
THE FORCE AWAKENS: VOLUME 4
WENDIG ROSS MARTIN

Hardcover Book ISBN
978-1-5321-4025-9

STAR WARS
STAR WARS
THE FORCE AWAKENS
THE FORCE AWAKENS: VOLUME 5
WENDIG ROSS MARTIN

Hardcover Book ISBN
978-1-5321-4026-6

STAR WARS
STAR WARS
THE FORCE AWAKENS
THE FORCE AWAKENS: VOLUME 6
WENDIG ROSS MARTIN

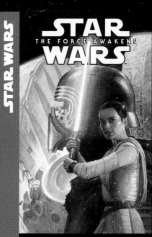

Hardcover Book ISBN
978-1-5321-4027-3